Playtime

A Girl Named Dan

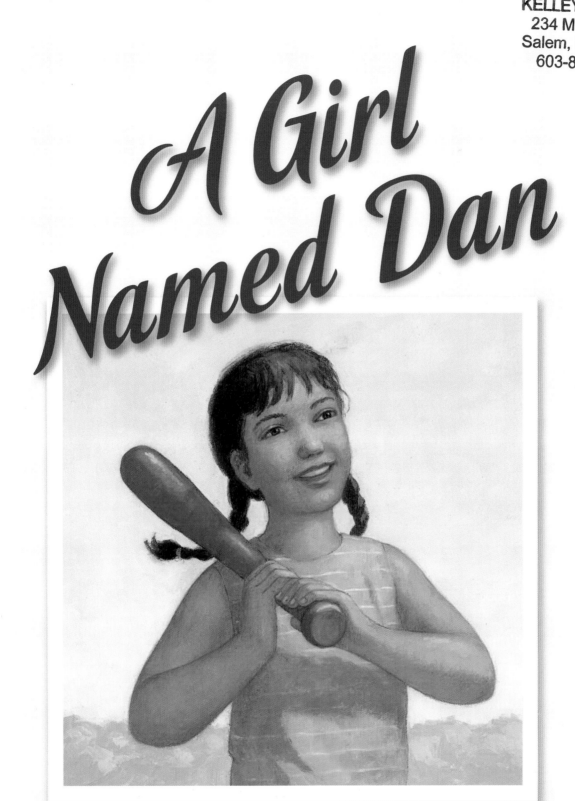

DANDI DALEY MACKALL

Illustrated by

RENÉE GRAEF

Definitions

Stan the man stance: the unorthodox batting stance Stan "The Man" Musial used during the last 15 years of his career with the St. Louis Cardinals

chin music: a high pitch, tight, right under the batter's chin

worm burner: a hard hit ground ball that "burns" the ground

shoestring catch: ball caught just before hitting the ground

slow bender: a long fly ball moving away from the outfielder

can of corn: a fly ball that is easy for a player to catch

napping: when an outfielder is slow to reach the ball

chasing junk: when a batter swings at a pitch outside the strike zone

beaned: when a batter is accidentally hit by a pitch

Text Copyright © 2008 Dandi Daley Mackall
Illustration Copyright © 2008 Renée Graef

Sleeping Bear Press®

310 North Main Street, Suite 300
Chelsea, MI 48118
www.sleepingbearpress.com

© 2008 Sleeping Bear Press is an imprint of Gale, a part of Cengage Learning.

Printed and bound in China.

First Edition

10 9 8 7 6 5 4 3 2 1

Library of Congress Cataloging-in-Publication Data

Mackall, Dandi Daley.
A girl named Dan / written by Dandi Daley Mackall
; illustrated by Renée Graef.
p. cm.
Summary: Dandi enjoys nothing more than baseball, and so after the boys at school tell her their lunchtime game is now boys only, she enters an essay contest hoping to become a bat boy for the Kansas City A's. Includes author's note on Title IX.

ISBN 978-1-58536-351-3

[1. Baseball—Fiction. 2. Sex role—Fiction. 3. Missouri—History—20th century—Fiction.] I. Graef, Renee, ill. II. Title.
PZ7.M1905Gir 2008
[E]—dc22   2007036615

*For all our family ballgames, and to our kids,
who still let us play with them—Thanks!*

—Dandi

For two Beste women, Donna and Donna.

—Renée

Author's Note

Title IX of the Education Amendments of 1972 was a 37-word law that said: "No person in the United States shall, on the basis of sex, be excluded from participation in, be denied the benefits of, or be subjected to discrimination under any education program or activity receiving federal financial assistance." It gave girls a chance.

Thanks in part to Title IX, my oldest daughter played school volleyball, my youngest daughter plays Special Olympics basketball, volleyball, and swimming. And they've both played softball, reminding me of a girl I used to know… named Dan. But things weren't always that easy for a girl.

In 1961 the whole world was competing against itself. Two major teams faced off—Russia and the United States of America. It was men who played in this big game, of course. Our side sent a secret spy who got shot down and captured by their side. Their team captain, Nikita Krushchev, got so mad at our team that he took off his shoe and pounded the table at the United Nations, shouting in Russian, "We will bury you!"

We all watched this on black-and-white TV and hoped it was just game chatter.

Turns out Earth wasn't a big enough playing field for these two teams. So the men took it to outer space. Russia sent up Sputnik satellites with dogs in them. So our new team captain, John F. Kennedy, promised we'd get a man up in space first.

We signed Hawaii to make fifty "United" States, but our team spirit wasn't the greatest. Martin Luther King kept telling all of us that black and white people were on the same team.

Not everybody was listening.

But the game went on….

For me, growing up in Hamilton, Missouri, population 1701 before the shoe factory closed, there was only one game that mattered. My daydreaming always lead me straight to the plate.

It's Game 7 of the World Series. The A's are down by three. Bases loaded. Two outs. Bottom of the ninth. "Up to you, Dandi!" come the cries from the K.C. dugout.

I crowd the plate with my "Stan the Man" batting stance.

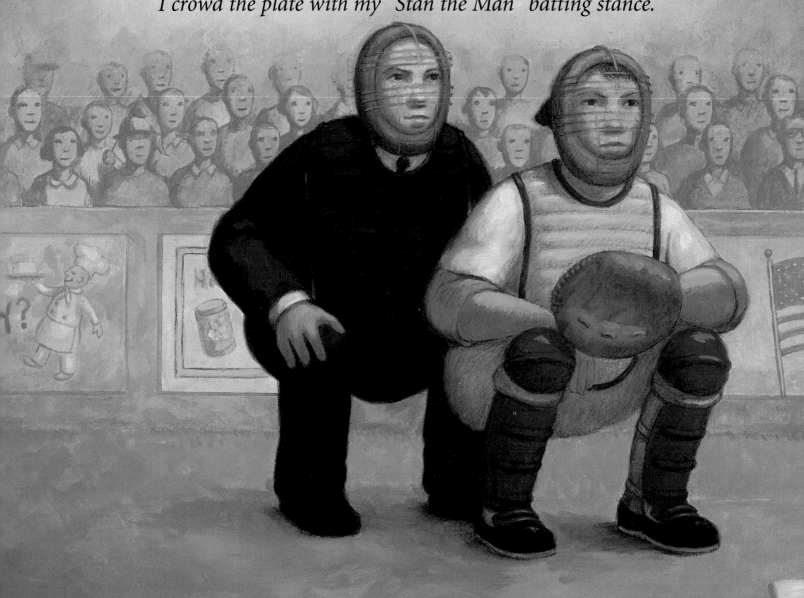

First pitch is high and inside, a little chin music to show me who's in charge. The next one catches the plate. I'm on it, but tip it back. The pitcher, worried, throws high heat for a 2-and-1 count. He jams me inside with a changeup. I have to hit. Foul ball. He throws low for a full count, 3 and 2. I foul off a worm-burner by third base. Then I see it coming—fastball, high, outside corner.

I know before the crack of the bat. The left fielder sprints to the wall, stops cold, and watches it go over the fence. A grand slam! The fans go wild. "Dandi! Dandi! Dandi!"

"Dandi!" Ray elbowed me.

"Who wants outside recess?" Mrs. Albertson asked.

Boys voted for outside, girls inside. Except me. We went outside.

Ray picked me fifth, even though the guys knew they could count on me to get on base. I may not have been a fence-buster, but I could "hit 'em where they ain't" every time. And I had good leather in the field, with speed for shoestring catches.

When the whistle blew, we were two runs up on Roger Steeby's team. I'd knocked in three runs on a slow bender and caught Roger's can of corn for their last out.

I raced home after school to change. It wasn't fair that girls had to wear dresses. By the time I got back, the guys were already in a pickup game.

I headed for the outfield, but Roger cut me off.

"You can't play," he said.

"How come?" I glanced over at Ray, who wouldn't look up from the mound.

"Because you're a girl. From now on, it's boys only."

Walking home, I fought off girl-tears. Nobody ever caught me napping like Wayne, or chasing junk like Roger did. But I couldn't play because I was a girl?

I hated recess without baseball. Instead of swinging a bat, I was forced to swing with girls and listen to talk about movie stars like Hayley Mills or teen idols like Fabian.

I still loved playing catch with my dad after dinner.

"Hey, Dan," Dad said, using my wish-you'd-been-a-boy nickname, "guess what Charlie O's up to now." Charlie Finley, the A's new owner, would try anything to get bigger crowds at games. "He's building a mechanical rabbit to pass balls to the umps. And he's having an essay contest to get batboys."

Something stirred inside me like when I was fixin' to steal a base. Batboy—for the Kansas City A's?

Saturday I took my Big Chief tablet outside, where I could hear mourning doves and barking dogs and smell alfalfa and clover.

Ray came over. He'd heard about the contest, too. We set to work side by side. I'd write something, then scratch it out. Write. Scratch. Write.

"Done!" Ray announced.

"Read it," I said, hoping he couldn't see how bad I wanted his to stink.

Ray stood up and read. "I really, really, really, really, really want to be batboy for the A's because they are so very, very, very, very, very, very good." He grinned. "It's not quite fifty words, but I can add more really's and very's."

Relieved, I burst out laughing.

"Oh yeah?" Ray shouted, pulling the entry form from his pocket. "Well, you can't even enter the contest!" He threw the entry at me before stomping off.

I smoothed it out. At the bottom, in tiny letters, it read: **For Boys Only.**

For days, I worked on my 50 words. Finally I had it:

Why I Want To Be Batboy

At the crack of the bat, I love that second of silence before boys, girls, parents, poor, rich explode with one voice. On a strikeout, I want to hear our groan, like we feel the same thing, so it's okay. We can't be so different if we feel the same.

I signed it "Dan Daley" and walked to the post office.

Time passed. Ray and the guys signed up for Little League. Boys only.

Then one morning, two men in three-piece suits showed up at my house. "Little girl," said the tallest guy, "we'd like to speak to your brother."

"Don't have a brother," I answered. "Want my sister?"

The short, bald guy popped open his briefcase. It had a Kansas City A's emblem on it. "We're looking for Dan Daley."

Dan Daley? My head felt like I'd been beaned.
Then I got it. "I won!"

I couldn't stop screaming. "I won! I'm a batboy!"

But the men weren't cheering. I panicked, afraid I'd been wrong. "Didn't I win?" I cried.

"You won," the tall man answered, still not smiling. "Only—"

"Only what?" I demanded.

"You're not a boy," he said.

He snapped his briefcase and muttered, "This was not a batgirl contest, little girl."

I didn't get to be batboy. Rules were rules. But a few days later I received an A's baseball cap in the mail. Then a jacket, which I stuffed in my closet with the hat because I'd become a diehard St. Louie Cardinal fan.

The next day a long box arrived from Kansas City. I knew what it was. I didn't want to open it, but I couldn't help myself. I slid it out, inhaled the wood, balanced it on my fingers, felt the carved baseball insignia.

I thought of all those bats I'd never hand to players—just because I was a girl. And I knew what I had to do. I grabbed the bat and headed for the schoolyard.

Just as I'd expected, the guys were all there—Roger at the plate, Ray on the mound. I never slowed as I scooched between Roger and home plate. "I'm batting," I said.

"It's a 3-2 count!" Roger protested.

"I'm batting," I repeated.

Ray knew I meant business because he motioned Roger back. "I'll pitch to her."

Anger surged through me as the first pitch came in high and outside. Gathering strength from every injustice, I—the girl who couldn't play—swung that bat.

There was a crack as bat met ball. I got a glimpse of boys in the field, heads back, mouths open, as my ball sailed over their heads, over the fence, across the ditch, across the road, and into the Bergers' yard, where no ball had ever gone before.

I rounded the bases as if I did this every day, tagged home, then kept going.

"Dandi!" Roger shouted. "You forgot your bat!"

Without turning, I replied, "Let the batboy bring it."

That year the Yanks took the Series in Game Five. Roger Maris smacked a 2 and 0 pitch into right field for his 61st homer, beating out Mantle and breaking Babe Ruth's record. America got men into space, and President Kennedy promised we'd put a man on the moon. Russia started building the Berlin Wall to keep our side out and theirs in.

The A's finished dead last in the American League, and I didn't much care. I played ball with my dad and cheered for the Cards. And I kept writing. I wrote about baseball. Then I wrote about dreams. I'm still writing.